# MORNING SONG

by Mary McKenna Siddals

illustrated by Elizabeth Sayles

• • •

Henry Holt and Company

New York

Henry Holt and Company, LLC
*Publishers since 1866*
115 West 18th Street
New York, New York 10011

Published in Canada by Fitzhenry & Whiteside Ltd.,
195 Allstate Parkway, Markham, Ontario L3R 4T8.

Library of Congress Cataloging-in-Publication Data
Siddals, Mary McKenna.
Morning song / Mary McKenna Siddals; illustrated by Elizabeth Sayles.
Summary: A young boy awakes and is happy to greet the day.
[1. Morning—Fiction. 2. Stories in rhyme.]
I. Sayles, Elizabeth, ill. II. Title.
PZ8.3.S5715 Mo 2001 [E]—dc21 00-57531

ISBN 0-8050-6369-2
First Edition—2001 / Designed by Martha Rago
Printed in the United States of America on acid-free paper. ∞
The artist used pastels and pastel pencils on paper
to create the illustrations for this book.
1  3  5  7  9  10  8  6  4  2

For my father,
Patrick A. McKenna,
who sang at my bedside
"Morning comes early, and bright with dew . . . ,"
and for my son, Sean—
my Morning Singer—
with love
—M. M. S.

• • •

For Jessica, of course
(with a special thanks to Alex S.
for his assistance)
—E. S.

Good morning, blankie.

Good morning, bear.

Good morning, bunny.
I see you there.

Good morning, eyes.

Good morning, nose.

Good morning, fingers.
There you are, toes!

Good morning, good morning,

good morning!

Good morning, pillow.

Good morning, book.

Good morning, baby.

Let's take a look.

Good morning, lamp.
Good morning, cup.

Good morning, clock.
Time to get up!

Good morning, good morning,

good morning!

Good morning, window.
Good morning, chair.

Peek-a-boo, sun!
I see you there.

Good morning, room.

Good morning, floor.

Good morning . . .

Who's that at my door?

Good morning,

good morning,

good morning!

Good morning!